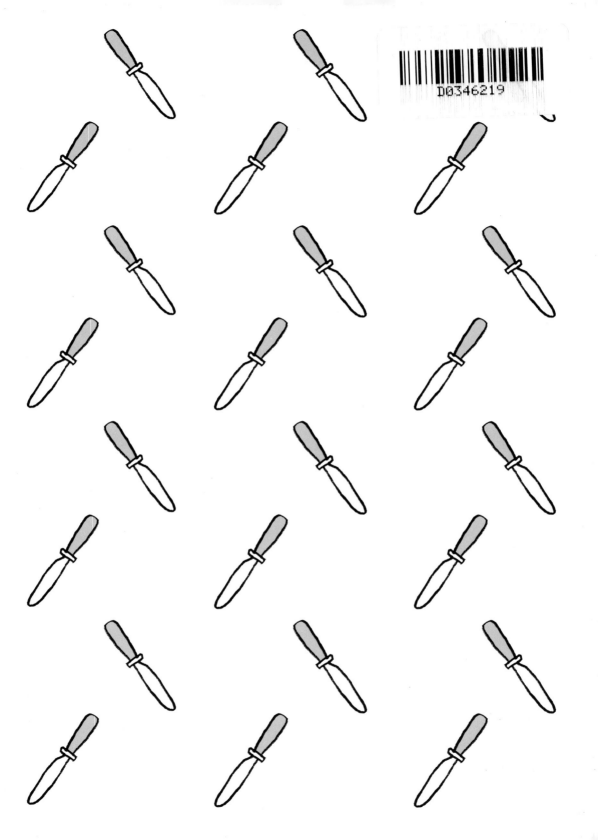

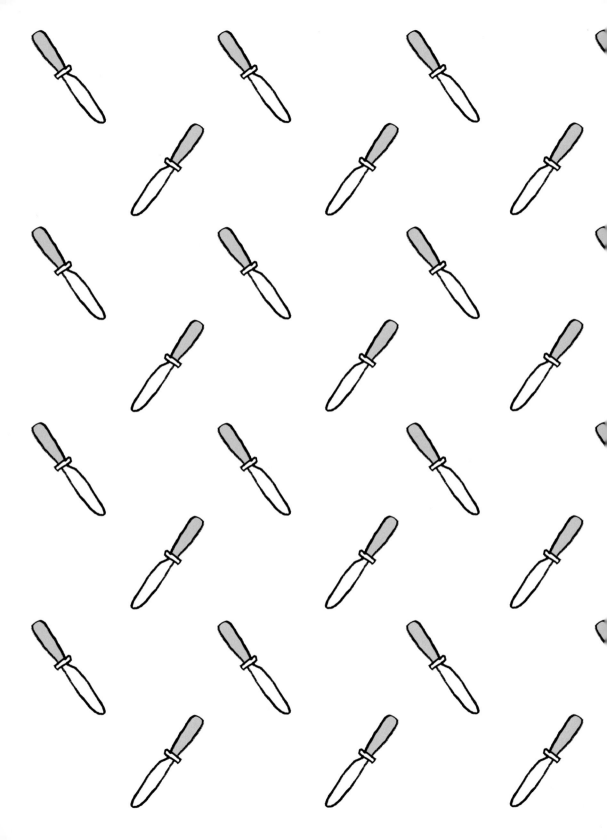

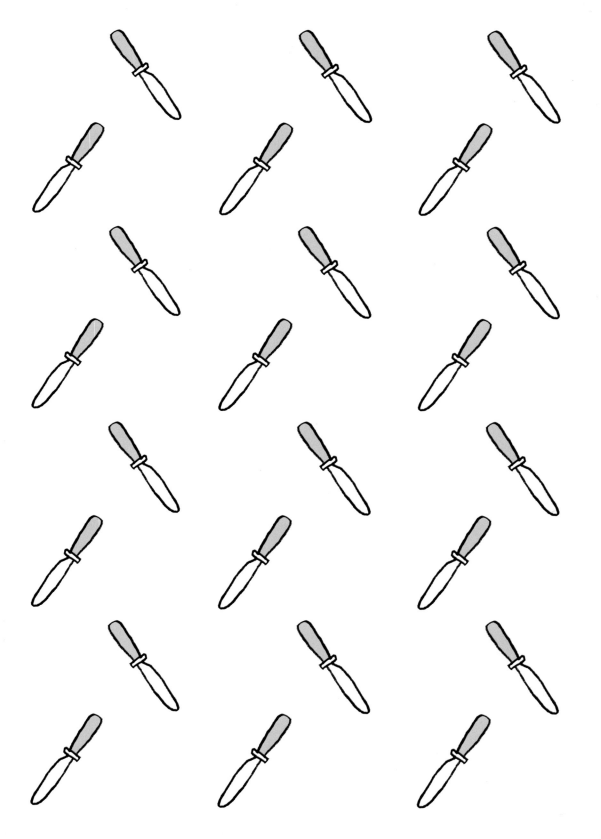

Pushkin Children's Books
71-75 Shelton Street
London WC2H 9JQ

Vitello Carries a Knife
Original Text: © Kim Fupz Aakeson and Gyldendal, 2008
Illustrations: © Niels Bo Bojesen and Gyldendal, 2008
English translation © Ruth Garde 2013
Published in the United Kingdom by agreement
with the Gyldendal Group Agency, Denmark

This edition published by Pushkin Children's Books in 2013

1 2 3 4 5 6 2015 2014 2013

ISBN 978-1-78269-005-4

Printed in China by WKT Co
www.pushkinpress.com

Kim Fupz Aakeson and Niels Bo Bojesen

VITELLO

carries a knife

Translated by Ruth Garde

Pushkin Children's Books

The boy called Vitello liked all
sorts of things. Loads of things.
Racing cars. Sweets. Bikes with
loads of gears. Cake. Stories
about zombies. Spaghetti with
butter and grated cheese. He
liked living in his terraced house
with Mum, and he liked funny
little dogs and lions. He liked his
annoying friends Max and Harry,
and he liked the little squirt
William. And watching films.

Yesterday he had watched a
brilliant film about this real tough
guy who had a big knife with
a jagged edge. The tough guy
wore a vest, he was as hard as
nails and was rude to everyone
and wasn't scared of anything.
Or anybody. There was also a
lady and some kissing, but
Vitello just closed his eyes
until that was over and the
lady had gone again.

Today Vitello wanted to be a tough guy, and be rude to everyone, and carry a knife. Without being scared of anything. Or anybody. And without any kissing. He started by putting on a vest. Then he found a knife in the kitchen. A brilliant knife. The bread knife. It was long and had a jagged edge. Almost like the tough guy's knife in the film.

"Don't even think about it," said Mum.

"I need a knife," said Vitello. "It's damn important."

"Mind your language. And that knife is sharp, so put it back in the drawer this minute," said Mum, and gave Vitello a butter knife instead. "You can play with this one."

"I'm not damn well playing," mumbled Vitello, but thought that a butter knife was better than no knife at all. He stuck it in his belt and set off on his quest to be a rude tough guy.

The sun was shining. Vitello stood
fiercely in the garden but he didn't
really know how to get started. His
neighbour was cutting the hedge with
some shears. His neighbour and his wife
and all their daughters were foreign and
from a different country. Mum called
them the Oddbods Next Door. The
neighbour said, "Hi little boy. Lovely
and sunny today."

"I'm not little, I've got a damn knife,"
said Vitello, and pulled out the knife.

"Very fine little knife you've got there,
hahaha," said the Oddbod Next Door.
"Little knife for little boy."

Hmmm, thought Vitello. You obviously
had to be even tougher to really hit
home.

Vitello strutted over to the little squirt William's house first and rang the doorbell. But nobody was home. There wasn't much point being a tough guy there. So instead Vitello strutted over to his annoying friends Max and Harry's house, and luckily they were home. Really home. They were playing in the garden with a stupid ball.

"Hi," shouted Max and Harry, who looked like two peas in a pod. "Shall we play football and be Barcelona?"

"I don't want to play with a stupid ball with you two little pipsqueaks," said Vitello, and stood so they could see his knife.

"We're older than you," said Max or Harry. "Four months older!"

"But in a pipsqueak-y way," said Vitello.

"On me head", said Max or Harry, to Max or Harry, and went on playing with their stupid ball.

"See you later, you snotnoses!" said Vitello, and took off.

"See you!" yelled Max and Harry.

Hmmmm. Obviously you had to be even tougher still.

Luckily, Vitello soon got the chance to be even tougher. He walked past a garden and a garden gate. And just on the other side of the garden gate stood a big white dog with yellow eyes. But today Vitello was carrying a knife, he was as hard as nails and he wasn't afraid of any dog behind any garden gate in the whole world.

Vitello looked at the dog and said, "What are you staring at, you stupid dog?" The dog growled. But tough guys couldn't care less. Vitello leant forwards towards the garden gate and said, "Blubba-lubba-lubba-lubba!"

Then that damn stupid dog went berserk.
It started barking its head off, and showed all
its white teeth. It barked like this: "WrrrrrOW,
wrrrOW wrrrOW!"

"I'm not scared of you," said Vitello and
pulled out his knife. "You should be glad you're
behind that gate, you stupid dog."

There was a small hole in the fence. Right
next to the garden gate. Vitello hadn't really
seen that hole. Not until now, when the stupid
dog started to squeeze through it to come and
sink his white teeth into Vitello.

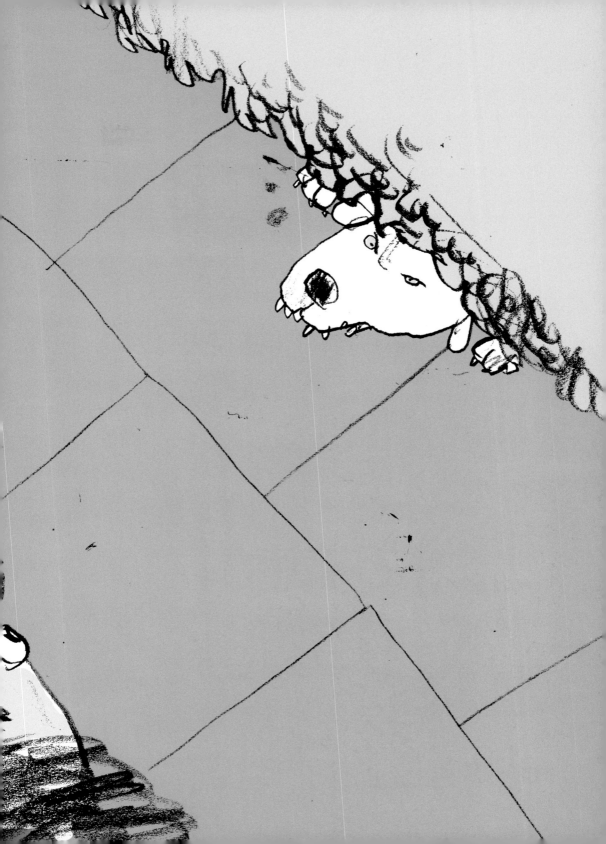

Vitello wasn't only tough. He was also good at running fast. That's what he did now, with the stupid dog chasing him. Luckily he was also good at climbing. He climbed over a low fence, took a short cut through a garden and came out onto another street.

And ran straight into a moped that was blocking the pavement. There were two big boys on all fours on the pavement in front of the moped smoking cigarettes and messing about with the engine. Their hands were filthy, and they managed to grab the moped before it fell over.

"Watch it, you little twerp!" said one of the big boys.

"I'm not damn well little," answered Vitello. "I've got a knife."

"That knife is a joke," said the other big boy, putting the moped back on its stand. "You total little twerp."

Vitello thought about what a tough guy would say, but it was hard to think straight, because that stupid dog wasn't so easy to get rid of. Right now for example it came tearing round the corner showing all its white teeth.

"Total little twerp yourself," said Vitello and sped off. Fiercely.

"WHAT??" shouted the big boys behind him. The dog barked; the boys yelled; Vitello ran.

Vitello ran round the corner and looked over his shoulder. The big boys were behind him and the stupid dog was just behind them. But luckily tough guys can run really fast, round another corner and round yet another corner. And straight into the tummy of a very very fat lady with a huge shopping bag and a walking stick and a silly hat with flowers.

"Look where you're going!" puffed the very fat lady, and shook Vitello hard by the arm.

"Lemmme g-g-go, you… you… hip… hip… hippo!" stammered Vitello, because the fat lady was shaking him so much he couldn't speak properly. "They're d-d-d-d-damn well after me!"

"WE'VE GOT HIM!" yelled the big boys.

"WRRRROWWW!" barked the stupid dog.

"DID YOU SAY HIPPO?" shouted the fat lady, and shook him even harder. The big boys now grabbed Vitello's other arm. The stupid dog tried to bite Vitello on the leg, but he was being yanked backwards and forwards so much that the dog ended up nabbing one of the big boys right on the bottom.

"OWWWWWW!!!" roared the big boy.

"HIPPO?!" bellowed the fat lady.

"LET GO OF HIM, YOU FAT COW!" yelled the other big boy.

"WRRRROWWW!" barked the stupid dog, with a mouthful of bottom.

"DID YOU SAY FAT COW?!" screamed the fat lady, and hit the other big boy with her walking stick.

And they pulled, and yelled, and hit, and bit, and pushed, and completely forgot the tough guy Vitello. Who ever so quietly crept away. Fiercely, of course, and also quite quickly, the whole way home along the hedges and indoors to the safety of his terraced house. Phew.

"Hi, sweetie," said Mum from the sofa. She'd had a glass of white wine and was watching a soppy film on TV. Maybe she'd had two glasses of white wine. Or three. And crisps.

"I'm not a damn sweetie," grumbled Vitello. Both his arms were really sore.

"But you're Mummy's sweetie," said Mum, and reached out to Vitello and pulled him towards her on the sofa. And kissed his hair. Vitello was just about to pull out his knife a bit, but Mum's arms suddenly felt so soft, and her smell of soap and crisps was so nice and there was nice music on TV. And then there was that kissing in his hair. Maybe it was hard to be a tough guy and be kissed at the same time. The boy called Vitello decided that he might as well put the knife down, and be a tough guy another day. And maybe not tomorrow, or the day after. There was no rush, after all.

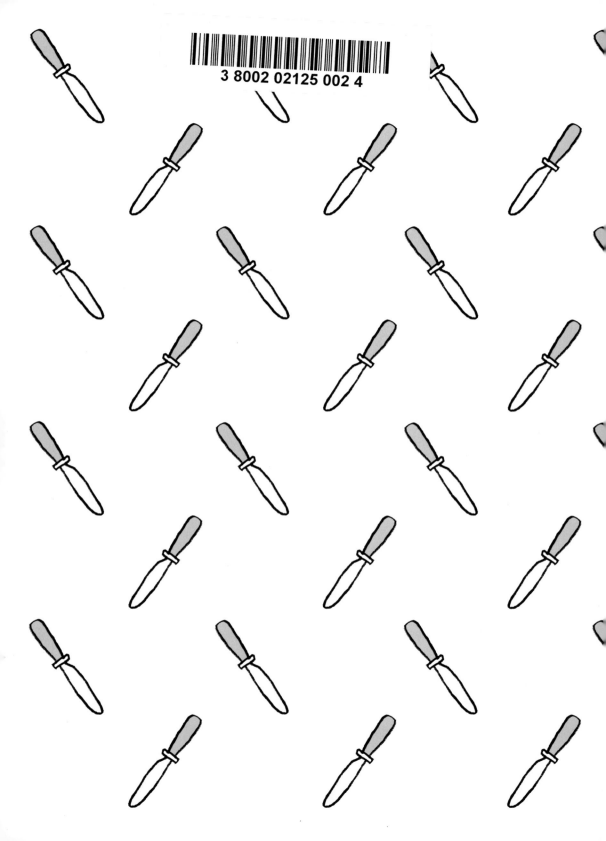

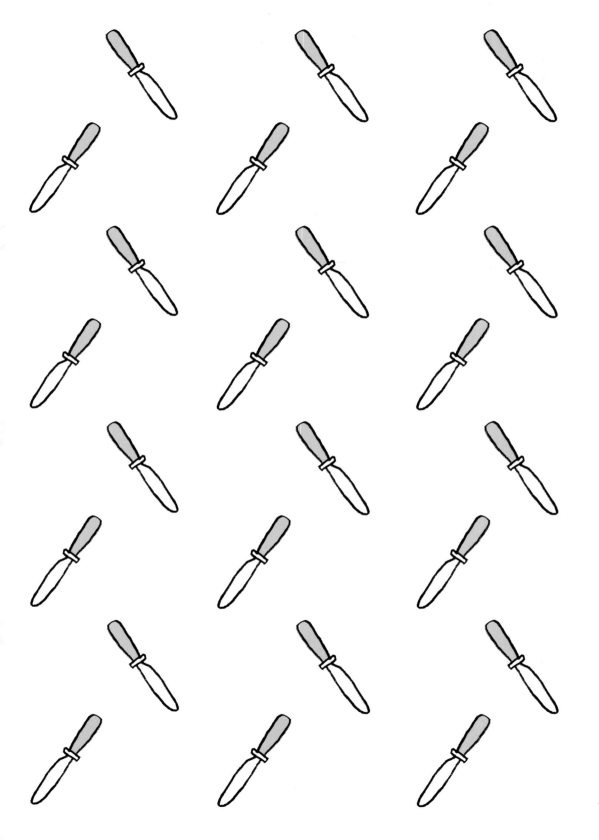

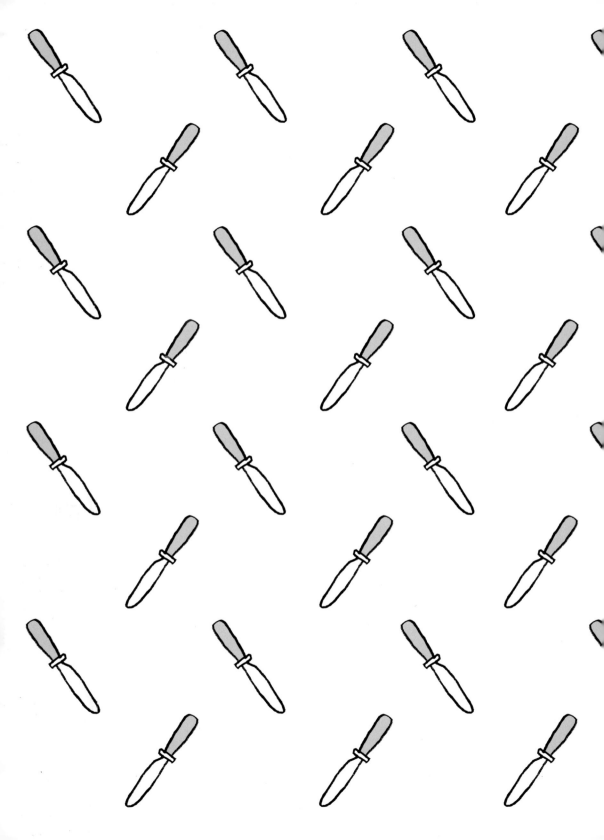